Sky Words

by Marilyn Singer

illustrated by Deborah Kogan Ray

Macmillan Publishing Company   New York
Maxwell Macmillan Canada   Toronto
Maxwell Macmillan International   New York   Oxford   Singapore   Sydney

Macmillan Publishing Company is part of the Maxwell
Communication Group of Companies. Macmillan
Publishing Company, 866 Third Avenue, New York, NY
10022. Maxwell Macmillan Canada, Inc., 1200 Eglinton
Avenue East, Suite 200, Don Mills, Ontario M3C 3N1.
First edition. Printed in the United States of America. The
text of this book is set in 12 pt. Meridien. The illustrations
are rendered in mixed media.
Library of Congress Cataloging-in-Publication Data
Singer, Marilyn. Sky words / by Marilyn Singer ;
illustrated by Deborah Kogan Ray. — 1st ed.   p.   cm.
Summary: A collection of poems about the sky and the
various phenomena seen there, including clouds, storms,
and sunsets. ISBN 0-02-782882-4   1. Sky—Juvenile
poetry.   2. Children's poetry, American. [1. Sky—Poetry.
2. American poetry.]   I. Ray, Deborah Kogan, ill.
II. Title. PS3569.I546S59 1994   811'.54—dc20
92-3765

10   9   8   7   6   5   4   3   2   1

To Judith Whipple, with thanks—M.S.

For Nicole—D.K.R.

*Thanks to Steve Aronson, Nora Chavooshian,
Kathleen Cotter, and Joe Morton*

Skywriting

I want to be a pilot
    writing messages in the sky
Mysterious white words
    stretched wide between the clouds
that disappear in moments
    like letters printed in invisible ink
I want to make the man with the jackhammer
        the kid with the balloon
        the gardener
        the sunbather
        the first baseman
        the cop
All stop what they're doing
    look up at the same time
    and smile at this magic in the air
Then later wonder
    if it really was there

Meteor

This rock
    they say
it fell
    from outer space
This rock
    as heavy as five thousand smashed cars
Whooshless
    it fell
      through the blacky black
        until it got to the sky blue
          then, whew!

At the Fair

Sara dared me
    so I had to
After the caterpillar
    and the carousel
Before the cotton candy
    and the lemonade
Sara dared me
    so I had to go
        on the scariest ride
           at the fair
Red and gold in the air
    it hung
It swung
    up and down round and round
        like a giant's hammer
           covered with jewels
Sara and I stubborn as mules
    got Uncle Steve to take us on
Up and down round and round
    we swung
        till we didn't know the earth
           from the sky
Uncle Steve was laughing
Sara was screaming
I wished that I was back home
    dreaming
When we got off at last
    we were kind of unsteady
Except for Uncle Steve
    who said he was ready to do it again
But Sara said, "We're hungry"
    and grabbed me by the hand
    and giggling we wobbled
        to the nearest hot dog stand

When the Tornado Came

It rained frogs
    when the tornado came
Big-mouthed bullfrogs
    all over the road
And a load of tadpoles too
    from Wilbur's pond
We were scared
    when the tornado came
In the cellar
    we huddled
singing that Christmas song
    about the partridge in the pear tree
We sat there so long
    that when we left
the sky was laughing blue
    like nothing had gone wrong

Albatross

What would it be like
   to live in the sky?
To soar on long pointed wings
   through shafts of sunlight
   and lightning bolts
To look down at flying fish
          and freighters
          billows
          and blue whales
What would it be like to make everywhere
   and nowhere
          your home?
To roam
To wander over the southern seas
   on a lively breeze
   or a dead calm
To know a rolling stone
   gathers no moss
What would it be like
   to be an albatross?

Moondog

Some say there's a man in the moon
Some say there's a lady
But when the moon is full
I see a German shepherd in the sky
   always laughing
   never lonely
How could he be
   with the whole world
     lying at his feet?

Twilight

In the hour of the bat
     when the sky turns the color
       of an old man's hair
it's hard to stare
Your eye stutters
     when something flutters
       like a scrap of silk
         on a vagrant breeze
           among the shadowy trees
In the hour of the bat
     when the world fades like a photo
       left lying in a drawer
though it's happened before
still
     you always get a chill
And you have to close the shutters
     you have to lock the door

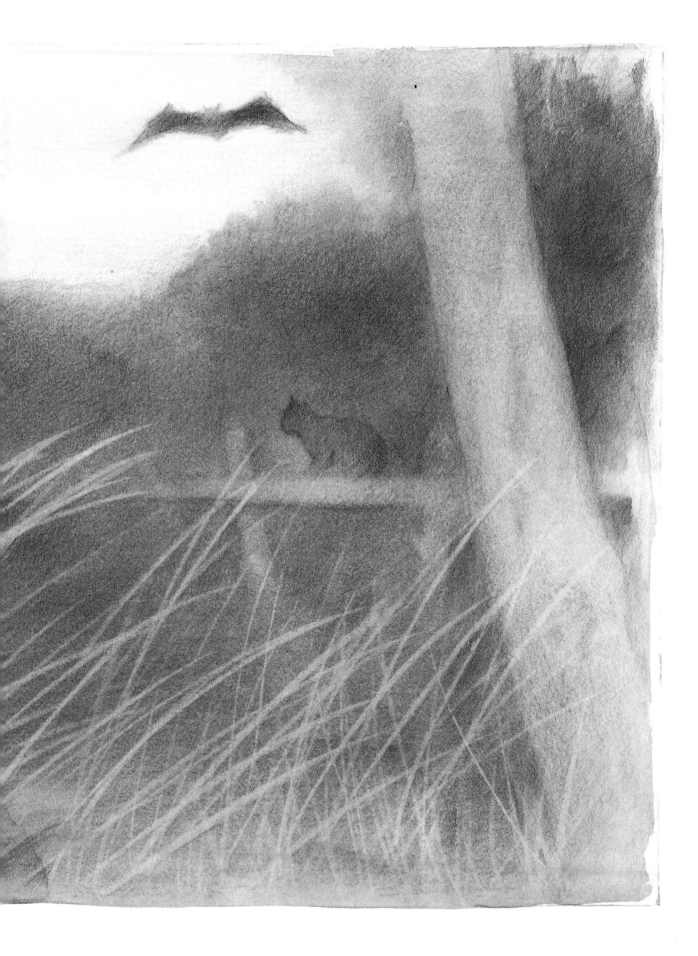

The Names of Clouds

Grandpa and Grandma argue
    over the names of clouds
"Cirrus. Cumulus. Cirrocumulus," he says
"Mares' tails. Cauliflower. Mackerel sky,"
    says she
Then the sky gets thick and dark
    and the wind begins to blow
"Cumulonimbus," Grandpa declares
"Thunderheads," Grandma insists
"Storm!" I shout
    and we run ahead of the rain
        into the dry red barn

Housekeeping

I used to think
    when I was smaller
that it was Mama
    who arranged the sky
That she went out each day
        at dawn
        in her old blue bathrobe
        to set the neat round sun
            above the horizon
        and put the clouds
            carefully in place
just the way she laid the table
        every night
            for supper
Once I hid behind the holly bush
        by the back door
and watched its berries go
        from black to purple
            to good morning red
            as the sun came up
                all by itself
And I thought Mama must be taking
        the day off—
it's another mother's turn today
Then I sneaked back to my bedroom
        determined to catch her
            some other time
                at her earliest morning chore
But of course I never did

Sometimes

Sometimes the clouds need a washing
    Sometimes the blue is too cold
Sometimes the sun's only joshing
    Sometimes the moon looks so old

Sometimes a rainbow surprises
    Sometimes the fog looks like lace
Sometimes the stars wear disguises
    Sometimes it rains on my face

But only in July
    have I seen a mustard sky

Monarchs Migrating

Sitting on my roof
    one shining September day
I thought some tall tree
    had gotten tired of summer early
      and sent its orange leaves
       into the sky
Then I stared as one sailed by
    A leaf with wings—
      a butterfly
A whole flock of monarchs heading south
    before the birds
    before the fall
      feeling winter's distant call

Fog

Trees have no tops
    in the fog
Bridges have no bottoms
Steeples rise like silent rockets
     frozen in space
Street lights float
    like UFOs
No one is your friend
    in the fog
The sky is a liar
The ground is a sneak
All footsteps belong to strangers
     even your own
The fog is
    a river with no direction
    a dream with no doors
When it lifts without a whisper
    you forget that it was ever there
        except for a tiny tickle in your mind
           a trace of goosebumps
            on your skin

In the City

Between the big buildings
    the sky
is served up in wedges
    like pie
For all of the folks
    on the ground
there isn't enough
    to go round

Astronomy

The stars don't stay the same
    outside my window
The one I wish upon in autumn
    has gone away in spring
Those constellations that chased across
    the Christmas sky—
        the hunter
        the dogs
        the bull—
are racing somewhere else
    on Independence Day
Light years away
    nebulae give birth to stars
    planets wander
    whole galaxies come and go
        turning and turning
        like the hands of the clock
        I glance at once in a while
If I watch long enough
        hard enough
could I catch them moving?
Could I see each tiny step
    they take every moment
        every night
    until they dance clear
        out of sight?

December 31

On New Year's Eve in the park
   we stand dozing
     on the frozen grass
People pass with shiny hats
   and hushed horns
     eager, waiting
Then someone shouts, "Countdown!"
And we wake at midnight
   to the clap and boom of fireworks
    showering bits of the sun
      through the deep, dark winter sky